THE LITTLE BROWN BEAR
AND
OTHER STORIES

The Little Brown Bear

and
Other Stories

by
ENID BLYTON

Illustrations by
SUZY-JANE TANNER

AWARD PUBLICATIONS

ISBN 0 86163 144 7

Text copyright 1952 Darrell Waters Limited
Illustrations copyright © 1985 Award Publications Limited

First published 1952 as *Enid Blyton's Bright Storybook*
by Brockhampton Press Limited

This edition entitled *The Little Brown Bear and Other Stories*
First published 1985
Third impression 1988

Published by Award Publications Limited,
Spring House, Spring Place, London NW5 3BH

Printed in Great Britain

CONTENTS

1

Forgetful Fanny

'Oh dear! I forgot!' said Fanny.

She was always saying that. Then she would go on: 'I'm so sorry. I did mean to remember, but somehow I forgot!'

Sooner or later everyone was cross with forgetful Fanny. Mother was cross because she forgot to post the letters and they were in the pocket of her coat for days. Daddy was cross because she forgot to shut the shed door and somebody got in and stole his best spade. Aunt Mary was cross because Fanny forgot to call in at the paper shop and bring back her paper for her.

And her teacher was cross because she forgot almost everything! 'Fanny! Why don't you use your memory? You simply don't *try* to remember! It's surprising to me that you remember to dress in the mornings, and to have your breakfast and come to school!'

Fanny was eight. Soon she would be nine. 'Can I have a party, Mother?' she asked. 'Let me see - when is my birthday? I've forgotten the exact date.'

'What a child!' said Mummy. 'It's on the fifth of May. Yes, of course you can have a party.'

'And a birthday cake, Mother?' asked Fanny.

'Yes, a big birthday cake – and ice-creams for everyone!' said her mother. 'And Fanny, perhaps when you are nine you will remember things a bit more, and not be so careless and forgetful!'

Fanny told everyone about her party.

'I'm to have a beautiful big birthday cake with nine candles on it, and there are to be ice-creams for everyone!' she said. 'You are all to come, all in my class.'

Mother looked in her cupboard the next day, and decided that she hadn't enough things to make a lovely big birthday cake. Sugar was short, and there were no birthday candles to be had, and Mother hadn't any cake decorations.

'I think we will ask the baker to bake you a birthday cake,' she said to Fanny.

'We can order the ice creams there, too. Let me see – how many of you will there be, Fanny?'

'Eighteen,' said Fanny. 'Oh, Mother – can the baker decorate my cake with sugared violets and silver balls? I would so much like those. And can we have strawberry, chocolate and vanilla ice-cream, all in layers?'

'You can,' said Mother. 'I'll write a note to the baker and tell him exactly what we want. He can deliver the cake and the ice-creams at four o'clock in the afternoon of your birthday, when the party has begun.'

So the note was written, ordering the beautiful birthday cake and the ice-creams. What fun! Mother stuck down the envelope and wrote the address.

'You can take it to the baker yourself,' she said. 'You are going out to get yourself some sweets, aren't you? Well, then, you pass the baker. So give it to him this morning.'

'Yes, I will,' said Fanny, and took up the letter. It was raining, so she fetched her mackintosh and her sou'wester. She stuffed the letter and her purse into the pocket and then she set off.

She bought herself some sweets and then saw a friend of hers, Joan Brown. Joan waved to her. 'Fanny! Come in a minute and see my new white mice! They're sweet!'

Forgetful Fanny

Fanny went into the shed to see them. It was warm and dry there, so she took off her mackintosh and put it on some sacks. Then she bent over the mice to see which one she liked the best. How sweet they were!

'Oh dear – I really must go,' she said at last. 'Hurray, the sun is shining! My goodness, Joan, is that the right time? I must run!'

So off she ran, and left her mackintosh behind on the sacks in Joan's shed! And in the pocket was the note to the baker! But Fanny had forgotten all about that!

On the next Monday it was her birthday. What a lot of presents she had, and what a lot of cards! Mother was busy making cakes and biscuits and jellies all morning whilst Fanny was at school. What a lovely party it was going to be that afternoon!

But, at four o'clock, when Fanny came running home from school with all her class, what a shock! The birthday cake hadn't arrived!

'Never mind – maybe the baker is sending it in a few minutes with the ice-creams,' said her mother. 'I'll send Jane down to see if they are ready, and she can bring back both the cake and ice-creams at the same time. You can all begin on the sandwiches.'

Soon Jane came back, puzzled. 'Oh, Ma'am,' she said, 'the baker's very sorry, but he says you didn't order either the cake or the ice-creams! So he hasn't got either of them for you!'

Fanny burst into tears! 'Oh, Mummy! A birthday party without a birthday cake! It's too bad! I did want to blow out my candles. Horrid, hateful baker! He just didn't bother!'

Mother was puzzled. 'Now, let me see – yes, I certainly did write the note for the baker, ordering the cake and the ice-creams. I wrote it last week. What did I do with it? Why, I gave it to you to leave with the baker, Fanny!'

Fanny remembered. 'Yes, so you did,' she said. 'Well, why didn't the baker make my cake then?'

'What did you do with the note, Fanny?' said her mother.

Fanny frowned. 'I put it into my mackintosh pocket,' she said. 'But I'm sure I left it at the baker's. I couldn't possibly forget to order my own birthday cake and ice-creams!'

'Where is your mackintosh?' asked her mother. 'Fetch it.'

But it was nowhere to be found. Then Joan spoke up. 'Oh, Fanny – do you remember coming to see my white mice? You had a mackintosh on then. Did you leave it in our shed?'

'Of course not,' said Fanny. 'I'm not as forgetful as that!'

'Oh yes, you are, Fanny,' said her mother. 'Jane, would you run down to Mrs Brown's and ask if Miss Fanny's mackintosh is in the shed there?'

Jane went. Soon she was back, with the mackintosh over her arm. Mother put her hand into the pocket – and drew out a letter! She turned it over and looked at the address.

It was her order to the baker! She

Forgetful Fanny

opened it – yes, sure enough, there was the letter, asking the baker to make a beautiful birthday cake, with sugared violets and silver balls on top, and nine candles round! And plenty of ice-cream.

'Well, Fanny,' she said. 'I'm afraid it is nobody's fault but your own that there isn't a birthday cake or ice-cream for any of you. You'll just have to put

up with home-made cakes and biscuits!'

'No birthday cake!' said the children. 'No ice-creams! Oh, Fanny – how *mean* of you to forget!'

The party was spoilt because Fanny cried all the time. The children went home early, cross and disappointed. Fanny sat in a corner and sobbed.

'Poor forgetful Fanny!' said Mother. 'This is the kind of thing that will always happen to you – if you don't try a bit harder to remember things. Poor forgetful Fanny!'

What a horrid birthday party! Do you think Fanny will go on being forgetful? She'll be very silly if she does!

2

The Little Brown Bear

Tony was very fond of bears. He had four toy bears: one very big brown one, one white one, and two small black ones. He liked books about bears too, and when he went to the zoo he wanted to spend more time looking at the bears than at any other animal.

'Tony's quite mad about bears,' said his mother. 'You'd think his big brown teddy was alive, the way he talks to it. And he's always asking me to give him a live bear for his birthday!'

Tony did like bears very much. He didn't know why. Girls loved dolls. He loved bears. He liked their plumpness and their blunt noses and little ears. The ones at the zoo looked as if they would like to play with him, but when he asked the keeper if he might go into the big yard and have a game with the bears, he said no, certainly not.

'Nobody will give me a pet bear,' said Tony. 'Nobody will let me play with one. I like my toy bears, but what I really want is a live one.'

One night, just before Christmas, he had a good idea. 'I know what I'll do,' he said. 'I'll ask Santa Claus for a real live bear for Christmas. Nobody can say anything against it if Santa Claus gives me one. I asked him for a train last Christmas and I got one. And I asked for a book about bears the Christmas before, and I got that too. So I'm sure I shall get a real live bear!'

He got some paper and a nice sharp pencil, and wrote this letter to Santa Claus:

19

'Dear Santa Claus,
 I am very fond of bears. If you can manage it, I should love to have one for Christmas. Thank you very much.
                    Love from
                        Tony'

He put it up the chimney in his bedroom, feeling rather excited. He told his mother and she laughed.

'Oh, darling, you know Santa Claus won't bring you a real live bear. He would know I wouldn't like one in the house.'

'Oh,' said Tony, disappointed. But when he went to look for his note up the chimney, it had gone. Probably Santa Claus had taken it. He wondered if he ought to write another one, saying he'd better not have a bear after all. But he didn't, because he felt sure Santa Claus would think him very silly if he kept changing his mind like that.

When Christmas morning came Tony couldn't help looking round his bedroom in great excitement, just in case there was a bear there. He looked under the bed and inside the cupboard. But there was no bear to be seen. He was sad, not surprised. It really was rather a lot to expect.

He had some lovely presents, though, and he forgot all about the bear that day. He had a new toy one, that could make a very deep growl, and he liked him very much.

The day after Christmas, Tony went out into the garden to play in the snow. He saw footmarks of the birds in the whiteness. He saw where Don, the old dog, had trotted in and out of the front gate.

And then he saw some more footprints that he really didn't know at all. Much too big for a cat. Not at all like a dog's. Certainly not a horse's hoofprints. Then *what* could they be?

He followed them. They came in at a gap in the hedge, went across a snow-spread lawn, and then went round a little shed nearby. Tony followed them round the shed. Then the footprints went in at the half-open shed door!

'Well,' said Tony. 'Whatever went into the shed certainly hasn't come out, because there are only going-in footprints, and not going-out ones. *Who* is in our shed?'

He pushed the door open wider and peeped inside. It was rather dark in there for there was only one small and very dirty window at one side.

The Little Brown Bear

23

Tony could see nothing except flower-pots, a barrow, some garden tools, and a heap of old sacks. But he suddenly heard breathing!

'Yes, something is breathing – under the sacks, I think!' thought Tony, and he stood very still. Then he saw that one side of the sacks was moving a little and – good gracious me! – what should poke out of the sack but a blunt brown nose!

Tony hardly dared to breathe. A wild thought came into his head. Was it a bear? Had Santa Claus actually sent him one after all? He stepped quickly up to the sacks and pulled them gently to one side.

And there, lying cosily curled up, was a little furry brown bear, his bright eyes looking up at Tony!

'Oh!' said Tony, in the greatest delight. 'You *are* a bear! And you're mine. A real live one. Santa Claus must have sent you here for me to find. He didn't send you to the house because he knew Mummy wouldn't like it. Bear, you are sweet!'

The bear yawned. Tony stroked his head and felt his little ears. The bear seemed to like it. He grunted and slid off the sacks. He lumbered over to Tony and rubbed himself against the boy's knees. Tony was so thrilled that he could hardly speak.

He went down on his knees and put his arms round the bear. 'You're mine!' he said. 'My own real live bear, to play with. I always wanted you. You are warm, you move, you grunt, you do everything you should. What shall I call you?'

The bear grunted again. 'I'll call you Grunty,' said Tony. 'It suits you. Dear Grunty, are you hungry?'

Grunty yawned again. Then he lay down heavily by Tony's feet, and began to lick his shoes busily.

'I'll just go and get you something to eat, Grunty,' said Tony. 'I won't be long.' He took his feet away gently and ran out of the shed. The bear didn't go with him. It just stayed there, waiting for the little boy to come back.

Tony went to find his mother. She was ironing, and was very busy. 'Mummy,' he said, 'what do bears eat?'

'Oh, buns,' said Mummy. 'And I believe they love honey.'

'Have we any buns?' asked Tony.

Mummy thought Tony was hungry. 'No, we haven't,' she said. 'But you can have some bread and honey if you like.'

'Oh, thank you,' said Tony, and went to get it. He cut four big slices and covered them with yellow honey. He put them on a dish and ran down to the garden shed. The bear was waiting.

He gobbled up the bread and honey greedily. Tony put down a bowl of water for him and he lapped that up too. Then he was ready for a game.

He played beautifully. He chased Tony, and Tony chased the bear. He growled and grunted, and pretended to be very fierce indeed. He didn't mind at all when Tony hugged him hard, and he tried to hug him back.

'Bears do hug, I know,' said Tony, pleased. 'Oh, Grunty, I wish I could take you to bed with me. But I can't, because perhaps I'd better not tell Mummy about you yet, in case she feels cross with Santa Claus. It would be dreadful if she sent you back.'

Mummy was surprised that Tony wanted to spend so much time in the garden, those December days, but she liked him to be out-of-doors as much as possible, so she was pleased. He rushed down to Grunty as soon after breakfast as he could. He took some of his Christmas money and bought six buns each day at the baker's. He bought a whole jar of honey, too, one day, and a tin of treacle the next. Grunty did so like sweet things. He liked the buns, too, and he even liked the dog's dinner, because once Tony found him eating it all up!

Don the dog didn't seem to like the bear at all. He kept away from him, and he whined when Tony tried to make him go with him to the shed to

The Little Brown Bear

make friends with Grunty.

One day Mummy went to the baker's for some biscuits. The baker gave her them, and said, 'Your little boy likes buns very much, doesn't he, Madam?'

'Does he? I don't think so,' said Mummy, surprised. 'Why do you say that?'

'Only because he comes here and buys six every day,' said the baker.

'Tony comes and buys six buns!' said Mummy, in astonishment. 'Oh, I think you must be mistaken.'

'No, Madam, I'm not,' said the baker. 'I know Master Tony very well indeed!'

Mummy went home, puzzled. Why should Tony buy buns every day? What did he do with them? He couldn't possibly eat six all by himself!

When she saw Tony she asked him. 'Tony, the baker says you buy six buns every day at his shop. Do you?'

'Yes, Mummy,' said Tony. 'I buy them out of my Christmas money.'

'Do you eat them?' asked Mummy.

'No,' said Tony.

'Then why do you buy them?' asked Mummy, more puzzled than ever.

'Well,' said Tony, and stopped. Now he would have to tell about Grunty. Bother! 'Well, you see – it's like this. I have to buy buns for my bear.'

Mummy looked as if she thought Tony had gone mad. His *bear!* What bear?

'What do you mean?' she said. 'Surely you are not giving your toy bears all those buns!'

'No. They are for my real live bear,' said Tony. 'You don't know about him, Mummy. He's the one I asked Santa Claus for, you know. And he sent me one. He lives down in the wood-shed, and I play with him every day. His name is Grunty, and I do so love him.'

Mummy got up. 'I simply can't *imagine* what you mean, Tony!' she said. 'Show me this bear, or whatever it is.'

'It *is* a bear,' said Tony. 'A nice furry one, real and alive.' He took his mother down to the shed, and opened the door.

Grunty came bounding over to him, grunting with pleasure, and rubbed his brown head against Tony's knee. He wasn't a very big bear.

'Good gracious!' said Mummy, stepping back, afraid. 'It *is* a bear! Tony, be careful. He'll hurt you.'

'Oh, Mummy – Grunty loves me,' said Tony. 'He'd never, never hurt me. I tell you, he's the bear that Santa Claus sent me.'

Mummy shut the door and took Tony's hand. 'Darling,' she said, 'I'm afraid it isn't a bear sent you by Santa Claus. There's a place not far from here where they bring up young animals and train them for circuses. I expect he has escaped from there. We must find out.'

Poor Tony! He wanted to burst into tears when Mummy said the bear might not be his. He went to the telephone with her, whilst she rang up the police-station to see if any bear had been reported lost from the training-place.

31

Yes, one had – the day after Christmas! Oh dear, it must be Tony's own little bear.

'I'm afraid it's your bear,' said Mummy. 'He's only a young one, and very gentle, so thank goodness he didn't hurt you – but Tony, dear, don't make pets of any bears you happen to meet another time, without asking me first! Really, I don't like to think of you keeping that bear for a pet, playing with him every day, giving him buns and honey to eat!'

Tony was very sad. When the man came to take Grunty away, he went up to him. 'May I say good-bye to Grunty?' he said, and his voice shook in a queer way. 'He was my own bear for a whole week. I do love him so.'

'Well, I never!' said the man, as he saw Tony and Grunty hugging one another. 'Look at that! I say, young man, would you like to come up and make friends with all our young bears? It isn't often we get a boy that a bear likes as much as this one likes you.'

'Oh – *could* I come?' said Tony, his eyes shining with delight. 'Then I could see Grunty often. And all the other bears, too. Oh, yes, please, I'd like it better than anything!'

And so Tony didn't lose Grunty after all, but saw him three or four times a week, and played with him, and with all the other young bears, too.

'But I shall always like you best, Grunty,' he says to the little brown bear, 'because Santa Claus took you and sent you to our garden shed, and let you be mine. Weren't you surprised when he came along and fetched you on Christmas night?'

Then Grunty grunts loudly. You'd love him, I'm sure. It *would* be fun to have a real live little bear to play with, wouldn't it?

3

 *Hold Your Tongue!*

'I can't think why you let Tommy be so rude to you,' Daddy said to Mummy one day. 'He was rude at breakfast-time and at dinner-time – and I expect he will be rude at tea-time, too.'

'Oh, he doesn't mean to be,' said Mummy.

'But he *does*,' said Daddy. 'And he'll go on being rude till he's stopped. I won't have it. I shall whip him.'

'Oh, please don't do that,' said Mummy, who spoilt Tommy, and could never bear even to smack him. 'We'll think of some other way.'

'Well, if you don't stop his rudeness I *will*,' said Daddy. 'I know you love him very much – and he's a nice little boy – and he can be very sweet and good – and all the rest of it. But *I will not have a child of mine being rude to his mother.*'

Now, when Daddy spoke in that tone of voice he meant it. Mummy did hope Tommy wouldn't be rude at tea-time. She thought she would just warn him before-hand.

'Tommy,' she said, as he took his things off in the hall, 'do be a good boy at tea-time. Don't be rude to me, because Daddy doesn't like it. So please don't.'

Well, that wasn't the way to speak to a boy like Tommy, was it? It just made him feel all the ruder. What his mother should have said was: 'Tommy, one rude word from you and you go straight to bed and stay there. And that will happen *every time* you are rude.'

'Then Tommy would have hurriedly learnt a few good manners, and never been rude again. But some mothers are too kind and gentle for children like Tommy.

Tommy sat down to tea. 'Oooh!' he said. 'Chocolate cake! And jam sponge! But what's this jam, Mummy?'

'Blackcurrant,' said Mummy.

Tommy pushed it away. 'Blow!' he said. 'Why did you choose black currant? You know I don't like it.'

'Try a little,' said his Mother. 'It's nice.'

''Tisn't,' said Tommy, rudely. 'It's horrid.'

'If you can't speak nicely to your mother, hold your tongue,' said Daddy, suddenly.

Tommy didn't dare to be rude to his father. He didn't answer. For a minute or two there wasn't a word said by anyone. Then Mummy spoke.

'Did you get good marks at school to-day, Tommy?'

''Course I did.'

'Did you play football this afternoon?'

'Mummy, you never remember *any*-thing. You *know* it wasn't games to-day,' said Tommy. 'Really, if you were at my school you'd be at the bottom of the form, because you never remember anything!'

'I said, a minute ago, that if you couldn't speak nicely to your mother you must hold your tongue!' said Daddy, suddenly.

Tommy said nothing. He took a ginger biscuit. *'Put that down!'* said Daddy. 'Do as I tell you, Tommy, and hold your tongue.'

Tommy stared at him. What did Daddy mean? If he meant he was to be quiet and not say another word, all right, he wouldn't say anything!

'Well?' said Daddy, in a dangerous sort of voice. 'You're not doing what I told you to do. You're not holding your tongue. You know where your tongue is, don't you? Inside your mouth. Show it to me. That's right. Now put your hand to your mouth and take hold of your tongue. Hold it tightly so that it can't say any more.'

'But - but - I don't want to,' said Tommy.

'Well, you can choose,' said Daddy. 'Either you hold your tongue in the way I tell you to, or you come upstairs with me and I'll show you what happens to rude boys. You can choose.

But I warn you that I've got a special slipper up there that I've put ready to deal with you.'

Tommy didn't want to be spanked with that slipper. So he put his hand up to his mouth and held his tongue with his thumb and finger. It was slippery and wet, but he could just manage to hold it.

He sat there, holding it, his face very red indeed. 'He can't eat his tea,' said Mummy, sorry for him.

'That's his own fault,' said Daddy. 'I warned him he'd have to hold his tongue if he couldn't stop being rude to you.'

This was simply dreadful. There was all that lovely tea – but not a bit of it could Tommy eat because he had to hold his tongue. It is quite impossible to eat if you are taking hold of your tongue! You try it and see.

Tommy went without his tea. Mummy cleared away and Tommy got off his chair, angry and hungry. He let his tongue free and spoke to Daddy.

'Please could I leave go my tongue now? I won't be rude again.'

'Oh, yes, you will,' said Daddy. 'You've been rude to your mother for a long time now. You can't get out of the habit in a few minutes. You must hold your tongue till you go to bed.'

'But, Daddy!' said Tommy in horror. Daddy spoke sternly to him.

'Hold your tongue. Go on, hold it!'

And Tommy had to hold it. It was a most uncomfortable thing to do. He

40

couldn't play at soldiers, or get out his paints, because he wanted two hands for that. He couldn't even do his homework because it was drawing a map, and he needed two hands for the tracing. He felt very worried. He held his tongue with his left hand and wrote a note to Daddy with his right hand.

'What about my homework? What excuse shall I give Mr. Brown for not doing my maps?'

'Tell him the truth,' said Daddy. 'Just tell him you spent the evening holding your tongue. Nothing like telling the truth. Mr. Brown will certainly understand that you couldn't do your homework, in that case.'

'But everyone will laugh at me!' Tommy wrote on a piece of paper, still holding his tongue in his left hand.

'Do you good,' said Daddy, and that was that.

Tommy sat in a corner, holding his tongue, first with his left hand and then with his right. It was very tiring. And then, oh dear, who should come in

but Ted the airman, to see Daddy! Tommy thought the world of Ted. He had flown to America and back over a hundred times already.

Ted stared at Tommy. 'Hallo, youngster! Whatever are you doing?'

'He's holding his tongue, in case it says something rude,' said Daddy.

'Dear me!' said Ted, who had heard Tommy being rude to his mother, and thought it was a pity. 'Fancy having a tongue that behaves like that. I'm glad I can stop my own tongue from being rude, without having to hold it.'

Tommy felt as if he could burst into tears. It was miserable sitting there, holding his tongue, not being able to say a word, or do anything.

Ted went. Mummy came in with some sewing. 'Oh dear!' she said, when she saw poor Tommy. 'Daddy, how long is he going to do that?'

'Till he goes to bed,' said Daddy. 'I don't trust that tongue of his yet.'

'But he can't sit like that for *hours!*' said Mummy.

43

'He doesn't need to,' said Daddy. 'He can go to bed any time he likes! This very minute, if he wants to.'

Tommy stared at the clock. What, go to bed at a quarter to six like the baby next door? Still, what was he to do? He simply *couldn't* go on holding his tongue one more minute.

So he went up to bed. He couldn't kiss anyone good night because he had to hold his tongue till he got up to his room. How glad he was when he could let it go!

Daddy came up to see him when he was in bed. 'You brought that punishment on yourself Tommy,' he said. 'No decent boy must ever be rude or unkind to his mother. You happen to have got a gentle and generous mother, who isn't as strict with you as she should be. You should love her more for her gentleness, instead of taking advantage of it and being rude.'

'I know,' said Tommy, his face very red. 'I won't be rude again.'

'Well, if you are, you understand you

Hold Your Tongue!

will have to hold your tongue again,
don't you?' said Daddy. 'That's my
bargain with you. You can choose
rudeness and hold-your-tongue, or
politeness and talk-as-much-as-you-like.
Good night Tommy, and think it over.'

Tommy did think it over. He told his
mother he was sorry. He got better
manners quite suddenly, and nobody

ever hears him being rude now. What a good thing he had a sensible father!

4

They Can't Catch Brer Rabbit

'You know,' said Brer Fox to Brer Wolf, 'it's just about time we caught Brer Rabbit, Brer Wolf. He's getting so uppity these days, he'll soon be ordering us about!'

'Well, let's catch him, then,' said Brer Wolf. 'We'll think of a plan. Shall we set a trap for him?'

'I've got a better idea than that,' said Brer Fox. 'We'll catch him in a net!'

'How can we do that?' said Brer Wolf. 'He'll see a net.'

'Now, you listen,' said Brer Fox. 'We'll have a hunting party, see? You can bring a net to catch butterflies, and I'll bring one to catch fish. And we'll tell Brer Rabbit to bring a net, too, and catch what he likes. We'll say that we'll bring the lunch: he needn't bother to bring any.'

'And when he's not looking we'll clap our nets down over him – and that will be the end of old Brer Rabbit!' said Brer Wolf, pleased. 'A mighty fine idea, Brer Fox!'

Well, the two of them told Brer Rabbit about their hunting party, and Brer Rabbit listened with both his ears.

'You bring your net and catch what you like,' said Brer Fox. 'We'll bring ours, too. And don't you bother about any food, Brer Rabbit: we'll bring that, and we'll share it with you.'

'Well, that's mighty kind of you,' said Brer Rabbit. 'I'll be pleased to come. And don't forget I like carrot sandwiches, will you?'

Now, when the day for the hunting party came, Brer Rabbit made up his mind he'd be along at the meeting-place quite early. It seemed a bit funny that Brer Fox and Brer Wolf should be so friendly with him all of a sudden. So off he went early, and crawled under a bush to wait, taking his net with him.

Presently along came Brer Fox and

Brer Wolf, each with most enormous nets. 'Heyo, Brer Fox!' said Brer Wolf. 'My, you ought to be able to catch old Brer Rabbit in that! That net of yours is big enough to catch an elephant.'

'And yours is strong enough to catch a tiger!' said Brer Fox. 'Now, we must each pretend to be looking for fish or for butterflies as soon as we see old Brer Rabbit coming. You wait about by those flowers, and I'll sit down at the stream here. He's late.'

'Oho!' thought Brer Rabbit to himself. 'I'm late, am I? It's a good thing I was early, it seems to me!'

'Did you bring a picnic lunch?' called Brer Wolf to Brer Fox.

'Yes. I'll put it down here,' shouted back Brer Fox, and he put down a nice, fat basket of food, not far from Brer Rabbit's bush. The smell of it reached Brer Rabbit's nose, and it was very good.

Brer Wolf danced about among the flowers with his net, and Brer Fox swished about in the stream with his. They both kept an eye open for Brer Rabbit, but he didn't come, and he didn't come. He was looking through a hole in his bush at that picnic basket and wishing he could feast on what was inside it.

He waited till Brer Fox and Brer Wolf were looking the other way – and then he quietly pushed his net out from under the bush, and put it over the basket. He began to draw it back towards the bush,.

He soon got it under the bush, and opened the basket. My, how good everything smelt!

'I'll take it home to my family!' thought Brer Rabbit. 'That's what I'll do!'

So, as bold as brass, he crept out from under the bush, and shouted at Brer Fox and Brer Wolf.

'Heyo, folks! Having a nice party? I hope you'll catch what you went to catch!'

Brer Fox almost fell into the stream when he heard Brer Rabbit shout. Brer Wolf stepped into some nettles and then out again in a hurry.

'Where did you come from?' shouted Brer Fox. 'We've been watching out for you for a long time. We wanted you to go hunting with us. You come here and see what I've caught.'

'I've been hunting under that bush,' said Brer Rabbit. 'You wouldn't believe what I caught!'

He swung his net around and Brer Fox suddenly saw that Brer Rabbit had got his picnic basket in it. He gave an angry yell and rushed at him. Brer Rabbit danced away.

'You're a thief, Brer Rabbit!' cried
Brer Fox. 'Yes, that's what you are!
You just came to steal our lunch. You

didn't come here to catch anything.'

'I did, I did!' shouted Brer Rabbit, dancing round and round a bush and making Brer Fox come after him with his net.

'Well, you tell me what you came to catch, then!' yelled Brer Fox. 'You just tell me.'

Brer Rabbit ran to the hedge and waved his net at Brer Fox. 'You go and catch fish, Brer Fox, and leave me to catch what I want to catch.'

'What are you going to catch? You tell me that!' shouted Brer Fox.

Brer Rabbit leapt right over the hedge. A bus was rumbling up the lane. Brer Rabbit put out his hand and stopped it.

'Heyo, Brer Fox!' he called, as he hopped up on to the step. 'I'm catching the bus. That's what I'm catching. *The bus!*'

And off he went with the picnic basket in his net, laughing so much that he could hardly put his hand into his pocket for the fare!

5

The Man Who Drew Faces

He was a very, very clever man. The children all knew him well, because he would often draw pictures for them. He could draw animals and toys and children and engines and ships and aeroplanes in the twinkling of an eye.

He had green eyes, and the children often wondered among themselves if he was a bit magic, because, as everyone knows, animals or humans with green eyes know quite a lot of things that other people don't.

The Man Who Drew Faces

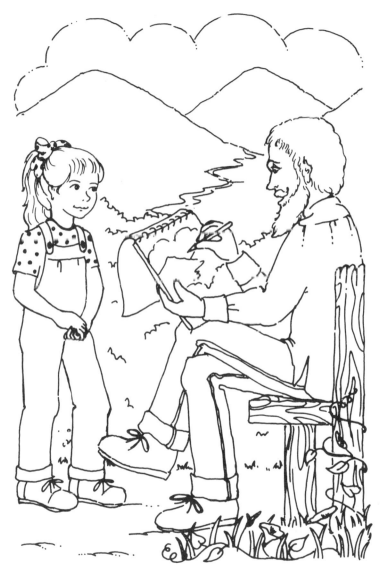

One day, little Sally Johnson found him all alone, sitting on a stile. He had his sketch-book on his knee and he was drawing the distant hills. Sally peeped over his arm.

'Can you draw faces?' she asked. 'You know – portraits of real people, so that I know who they are?'

'Oh yes,' said the artist with his green eyes twinkling. 'I'm very good at that, because I can draw what's *in* the faces, as well as the faces themselves.'

'What do you mean?' asked Sally.

'Well, now – who shall I draw for you?' asked the man, and he sharpened his pencil. 'You tell me – and you'll soon see what I mean.'

'Draw my Granny's face,' said Sally.

The man set his pencil to his paper and began to draw a face. It was a lovely face, sweet and young.

'That's not my Granny!' said Sally.

'It is – when she was twenty,' said the artist. He put in a line or two – and then some more. He gave the mouth a little twist, and drew wrinkles round

The Man Who Drew Faces

the eyes. The face became old and rather sad and tired.

'Yes. That's my Granny,' said Sally. 'You made her into my Granny when you put in those little lines. How funny that those tiny lines should make that face into my Granny's!'

'They weren't always in your Granny's face,' said the artist. 'See that one, there – that's a worry line – it came when one of her sons ran away and didn't write to her for two years. And do you see that one – that little frown line? That came when your Grandpa lost his money, and she was cross and upset because she had to give up her nice house and garden, and hadn't much money to bring up her children.'

'Yes. Mummy told me about that time,' said Sally. 'Did it really put that line into her face? What's that one – at the corner of her mouth? It's a nice line – it makes her mouth look sweet.'

'Ah, your mother put that there!' said the man. 'She was good and sweet and helpful, and your Granny couldn't help smiling when she was about.'

'Oh, I'm glad,' said Sally. She pointed to the wrinkles. 'Look at those lines. How did Granny get those?'

'They came when one of her daughters was very ill,' said the man. 'And they got worse when your Granny discovered that a great friend of hers was doing something wrong. And they got worse still when she felt ill, and was always cross with people. It's a good face, isn't it, though – even though it's a bit tired and sad?'

'Yes,' said Sally. 'I didn't know people's faces grew like that because of things that happened to them. Now draw my mother's face. She's lovely.'

The man drew another face, round and young and unlined. Sally knew it was her mother when she was younger. 'You haven't put in the lines,' she said. 'Mummy hasn't many, but she's got a few. Add them in and tell me what they mean.'

'Well, here's one,' said the artist. 'That came when your brother fell off his bicycle and broke his leg very badly. That's a worry line. And here's another. That came when your Granny was very ill – that's a very sad line, isn't it?'

'Yes. But Granny's better now, so perhaps that line will go,' said Sally. 'I

don't like it. It makes Mummy's face look old. What are those little lines round her eyes?'

'Oh, they're laugh lines,' said the artist. 'Your mother's fond of a joke, isn't she, and she's gay and bright. She put those merry little lines there herself. But here's a bad line, look – now what was that? Yes, it was when your big sister wouldn't work at school, and almost got expelled for her naughtiness.'

'Yes. I remember that, though I was very small then,' said Sally. 'But Janey's better now – she's just won a scholarship. That line oughtn't to be there any more.'

'Janey put it there, and there it will stay,' said the artist. 'It would make Janey very sad if she knew.'

Sally looked earnestly at the picture. Yes, it was her mother's face, there was no doubt about it. She looked at a dear little curly line by the mouth. 'What's that?' she said. 'I like that. What put that nice little smiley line there?'

63

'You did, Sally,' said the artist, and his eyes looked very gentle. 'You're a nice little girl, you know – and I've heard you're sweet-tempered and kind. The only line in your mother's face that you've put there is that little curly one you like – and see – I'll make it a little bigger – and now your mother's face is even sweeter.'

'Yes. It is,' said Sally. 'I'll make it bigger on Mummy's *real* face. You see if I don't! I'd like to give Mummy a nice smiley line like that. I'd really love to put that into Mummy's face. Do you think people know how faces are made – do you think. . .?'

'Oh, I can't answer so many questions!' said the artist, and he got down from the stile. 'You want to know too much! I've given a lot of secrets away to-day. Good-bye, Sally. Use my secrets well!'

I'd like to meet that green-eyed man, wouldn't you, and see him draw some faces? I wonder what lines you've put into your own mother's face? Some very nice ones, I hope!

6

Santa Claus Gets Busy

Santa Claus was having a little snooze in his armchair on the afternoon before Christmas Day, when someone came banging at his door.

'Who is it? Didn't I say nobody was to. . .?' began Santa Claus, waking up with a jump. A little servant ran into the room.

'Santa Claus! Your reindeer are ill! Sneezing their heads off! They can't possibly take your sleigh to-night. You'll have to put off Christmas Eve.'

'Don't be silly!' said Santa, and he leapt up at once. 'Nobody can put off Christmas Eve. I'll come and have a look at the reindeer.'

But when he saw them he knew they couldn't pull his sleigh. They could hardly stand. He stared at them in dismay. '*Now* what am I to do? Can't disappoint all those millions of children!'

'Go in a helicopter,' said the stable-man. 'It's easy to land on roofs in that.'

Santa Claus snorted like a reindeer. 'A helicopter! What next? I don't go in for these new-fashioned things. I'm old-fashioned and I like reindeer for Christmas Eve. Now – where in the world can I get some?'

'I saw some once in the London Zoo,' said the stable-man, wiping a reindeer's nose for him. 'Not so good as these. Still, they might do. You'd have to ask the keeper though.'

'I will!' said Santa Claus. 'Get him on the telephone at once.' So, to the enormous astonishment of the reindeer's keeper at the Zoo, Santa Claus talked down the telephone to him, and suggested that he should lend him four of his best reindeer in a few hours' time.

'Don't be funny,' growled the keeper, who didn't believe in Santa Claus. 'I don't like this kind of joke.'

Santa Claus was angry. 'What's your name?' he snapped. 'John Robins?

Wait a minute. I'll look you up in my Christmas book. Yes, here you are – twenty-five years ago you were a little boy living in Jasmine Cottage, Ardale. That right?'

'Er – yes – that's right,' said the keeper, puzzled.

'And one Christmas you badly wanted a toy farm and called up the chimney to ask me for it, didn't you?' said Santa

Claus. 'And what's more, I heard you, and brought it. I put the farm at the end of your bed and filled your stocking with the animals and the farmer. Do you remember? *Now* will you believe I'm Santa Claus, and lend

me four of your reindeer?'

By this time the keeper was so puzzled and scared that he was ready to agree to anything. 'Well, listen,' said

Santa Claus. 'Get them out at once. Say one word into their ears – annimal-oolipatahmekaroo. Got it? Repeat it after me. It's a magic word that all reindeer know. I'll send a messenger with some fly-paint for their heels.'

'Fly-paint?' said the keeper, faintly.

'Yes – fly-paint to make them gallop up into the air,' said Santa Claus, impatiently. 'I'll send them back safely when I've finished with them. Thanks very much.' He slammed down the telephone receiver and blew out his cheeks. 'Done it! Where's Pip? Send him straight to the Zoo with the paint for the reindeer's hooves.'

In two hours four magnificent reindeer came galloping through the evening sky to the castle of Santa Claus. The keeper had groomed them beautifully, and had even polished their antlers with furniture polish. He felt as if he were in a dream as he whispered 'annimaloolipatahmekaroo,' but when he saw the reindeer at last galloping up into the air, he couldn't

help feeling pleased and excited. 'I must tell my little boy,' he said. 'He won't believe me, but I really must tell him.'

The toys were all ready packed into Santa Claus's sack. They made their usual yearly grumble about being too squashed for words, but Santa took no notice of that. At exactly the right moment he rose into the air, his great sleigh pulled easily along by the four Zoo reindeer. Bells jingled madly, and Santa Claus held on to his hood, and pulled at the reins.

'Hey! Not so fast! There's a speed-limit for reindeer.'

They slowed down a little. They were proud and excited, and it was a long time since they had had a real gallop. They were good and intelligent animals, and only made one mistake. That was when one of them accidentally put his hoof through a sky-light on a roof, and broke it. Santa Claus's own reindeer never did a thing like that. They were too well-trained.

'Never mind, never mind!' said Santa Claus. 'I'll put a special window-mending outfit into the child's stocking here. He'll enjoy that. Whoa now! You're just too lively for anything!'

Not a child was forgotten that night, and Santa Claus did the whole journey in record time, because the reindeer were so fresh, and so keen to show what they could do. They took him back to his castle at last, and he got down from the sleigh, his sack empty, tired out. He patted the reindeer, and gave them each a nose-bag full of reindeer moss.

'Hey, Pip!' he called. 'Take them

back when they've had a feed and a rub-down. Good creatures they are. That keeper ought to be proud of them. Oh, and Pip, slip down the keeper's chimney, will you, and put this into his little boy's stocking. I didn't think of it when I was there.'

He gave Pip four beautiful little toy reindeer pulling a sleigh with a tiny figure of himself driving it. 'And see that you wipe the fly-paint from their hooves *properly,'* he said. 'We don't want to hear of reindeer gadding about above the Zoo next summer. Though I daresay they would make a lot of money giving children rides through the air! Get along, now, Pip, and return the reindeer.'

Pip went off, riding the first reindeer, and leading the others on a rein. He set them all safely down in their quarters at the Zoo. He slipped down the keeper's chimney and left Santa Claus's present in the child's stocking. Then he took a duster from his pocket and went to rub off the fly-paint from the hooves.

But wait a minute – hey, Pip! Come back again. You've forgotten one of the reindeer – he's still got the paint on his hooves. But Pip's gone. Well, well – that means a bit of excitement at the Zoo one day next year. I hope I'm there to see it!

7

The Little Girl Who Was Shy

There was once a little girl called Janet who was very shy. She was so shy that she couldn't even shake hands, or say 'Quite well, thank you,' when people spoke to her. And even if people asked her how her dolls were, or if she liked sweets, she still didn't say a word.

I expect you think that's rather silly, but perhaps you are sensible enough not to be shy. Janet wished and wished she wasn't shy, but she just *couldn't* seem to make her tongue talk when visitors came. Mummy was quite ashamed of her.

Now one day Janet went out with her Auntie. They went into the fields, and Auntie sat down with her back against a tree to do some sewing.

'You run about and play,' she said to Janet. Janet ran off a little way and then came back to show Auntie something she had found.

But her aunt was fast asleep! Janet didn't like to wake her up. She ran off again – and suddenly, just behind a big blackberry bush, she saw about twelve very small people. They were all walking along, talking in tiny high voices, rather like the swallows do.

Janet stared in great surprise. She thought they must be fairy-folk, they were so small. They looked up at her and smiled.

'Good afternoon,' said a little fairy girl. 'What's your name?'

Well, of course, Janet was too shy to say her name! She just went red and said nothing.

The Little Girl Who Was Shy

'We are going to Jinky's birthday party,' said another fairy. 'Would you like to see what I'm taking him for a present?'

Janet was simply longing to see the present, but her tongue wouldn't say a word.

'Would you like to come with us, little girl?' said a third little person. 'Jinky would like to see you.'

Well, Janet would have liked that better than anything else in the world – but she still didn't answer. Then the fairies began to talk to one another in surprise.

'She doesn't speak! She doesn't say a word!'

'Do you suppose she has a tongue?'

'Poor little girl! She can't talk. And she looks such a dear little girl too. What can we do about it?'

'Have you a tongue, little girl?' asked the first fairy. Still Janet didn't answer. She really was a little silly, wasn't she?

The fairies talked again. 'We can't give her a tongue, because she's so tall and big. We'd never reach up to her mouth.'

'Well, look at her shoes,' said another fairy. 'They are nice little lace-shoes – and they each have tongues! We could make those talk instead of Janet. Then, when people ask her questions, the tongues of her shoes can answer for her. That would be a help to her.'

Before Janet could take away her feet, one of the fairies had rubbed something on to the tongue of each shoe. Then they spoke to Janet.

'Can you speak now, little girl?'

And to Janet's enormous surprise, a voice answered from down near her feet – a funny deep voice. 'Yes, thank you. I can speak!'

It gave the little girl such a shock that she ran away at once. She ran to her aunt, who opened her eyes.

'Is anything wrong?' she asked Janet. Janet didn't like to tell Auntie about the tongues in her shoes being able to talk, so she said nothing. But the tongues answered at once.

'No, nothing is the matter, thank you, Auntie.'

Her aunt was surprised to hear such a deep voice. 'Why, it sounds as if your voice has gone down to your shoes!' she said. 'Come along now – it's time to go home.'

They went home – and Mummy had visitors! Janet was taken in to see them.

'Oh! So this is Janet!' said Mrs. Brown. 'How do you do, Janet?'

Well, Janet felt shy, of course, and

couldn't say a word. But that didn't matter! Her shoes answered cheerfully for her.

'I'm quite well, thank you!'

'What a well-mannered child – but what a deep voice!' said Mrs. Jones. 'And how are all your dolls, my dear?'

Janet didn't answer, but hung down her head. The tongues of her shoes spoke up well, quite enjoying themselves.

'Oh, my doll Angela has a bad cold, and is in bed. Josephine has the measles, and Hilary has fallen down and hurt her knee so that I had to bandage it.'

Now all this wasn't a bit true, and Janet felt really ashamed of her shoes for telling such stories. All the visitors laughed.

'Janet's voice seems to come up from her boots!' said Mrs. Harris. 'Well, my dear, what are you going to have for your tea?'

The shoes answered gaily. 'Sardine sandwiches, chocolate buns, ginger biscuits, and ginger-beer!'

'Oh, Janet! Don't tell such naughty stories!' said Mummy, quite shocked. 'You had better go back to the nursery. I do like you to speak when you are spoken to, but not to tell stories like that.'

Janet ran out of the room, angry with her shoes. On the way to the nursery she met Cook's sister, who had come to tea. Cook's sister liked children and she spoke to Janet kindly.

'And where have you been for your walk to-day, my dear?'

Janet was too shy to say a word – but the shoes spoke up at once. 'Oh, I went to the farm, and over the hill and down by the shops, and home by the fields – quite six miles!'

'Dear me!' said Cook's sister, surprised. 'That seems too long a walk for a little girl like you!'

'Janet! What stories!' said Auntie, who was in the playroom nearby. 'Why, we only went to the fields! Come along now and wash your hands for tea.'

Janet really felt very, very cross with her shoes. 'Next time anybody asks me anything, I'll answer before my shoes do, so that they can't get in their naughty stories first!' she thought. So, when a friend of Mummy's came in after tea and spoke to her, Janet answered at once.

'And what did you have for your tea?' asked Mummy's friend.

The Little Girl Who Was Shy

'Brown bread-and-butter and two biscuits,' said Janet at once, before the shoes could speak.

'There's a good girl, to answer so nicely,' said Auntie, pleased. 'You can have a sweet for that.'

Janet was delighted. She looked down at her shoes. The tongues wagged themselves a little, as if they were cross.

'Does Janet know her alphabet?' asked Mummy's friend. 'Could she say it to me?'

'She knows it very well – but she will never say it for anybody, she's so shy,' said Auntie.

Janet thought she had better say it at once, before her shoe-tongues said it all wrong. So she opened her mouth and said her alphabet beautifully. Auntie listened in the greatest surprise. Mummy's friend clapped her hands when Janet had finished.

'Clever girl! Here is tenpence for you! I never thought you could say a thing so nicely. I always thought you were rather a silly little girl before, who couldn't say boo to a goose!'

Tenpence! Janet was very pleased. She began to think that it was a very good idea to speak when she was spoken to, and to be polite and well-mannered. It was nice to be thought a clever, good little girl. And she just WOULDN'T let those shoes of hers say another word!

Well, you know, she didn't! As soon as anyone spoke to her all that week, Janet had an answer ready, and soon people didn't say any more that she was shy. They just said what a well-mannered, nicely-spoken child she was, and they gave her sweets and smiled at her kindly. Janet enjoyed it all very much.

'How silly I was to be shy!' she thought. 'It is much easier not to be. I never will be again – and those shoe-tongues will never, never get another chance to say a word!'

They didn't – and they were really very cross about it. When the shoes had to be mended next time, Mummy said she thought Janet had better have a new pair, because her feet had grown.

'We'll give these away,' she said. 'They are very good shoes still.' So the shoes were given away, and I do wonder if they went to a shy child. What a shock she will get, won't she, when the tongues begin to talk!

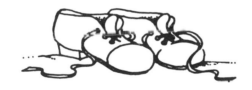

8

One Christmas Eve

'Can I go and look?' asked old Simon the fiddler. The vicar's wife and the children who had been helping her, turned round at his voice.

'Oh *yes,* of course, Simon,' said the children, and one of them took his hand. 'Have you got your fiddle this morning?'

'No. I've left it at home,' said Simon. 'Maybe I'll bring it to a Christmas party and play for you all to dance.'

The children ran off with the vicar's

wife. Simon went into the nearby church. He knew that the children had been making a little scene of the Nativity in a corner there, and that was what he wanted to look at.

He tiptoed in. He came to where the beautiful scene had been arranged by the children. He knelt down and stared at everything.

'It's lovely,' he thought. 'Just like the real thing must have been. There's the little stable with Mary and the little Christ-Child. There's Joseph looking after them. And they've even put the oxen in the stable too – and tiny doves on the rafters.'

It was a beautiful little Christmas scene the children had made. Outside the tiny stable they had made a hilly field, and some child had brought all his toy sheep to stand there. Shepherds huddled round a fire with their dogs. The dogs had been lent by little Jimmy Harries – he had a wonderful collection of toy dogs.

'The angels in the sky aren't there,'

said Simon. 'What a pity. The children should have put them there too.'

Simon wasn't very clever. Sometimes he was called Simple Simon. The children didn't mind how stupid he was, because he played his violin so beautifully for them. They loved the queer old man.

Simon didn't realise that it was too difficult for the children to arrange angels flying in the air above the little Nativity scene. He thought the children must have forgotten them. He knelt there for a long time, his bright old eyes taking in everything, even the little wisps of hay in the manger.

'The angels sang a song when they came that night,' thought Simon. 'I should have liked to play the music for it. A wonderful tune it must have been. What was it they sang? 'Peace on earth, goodwill towards men' - yes, that's how it went.'

On Christmas Eve Simon went back again into the church. He chose a time when nobody else was there - because he wanted to do something that perhaps people might not like.

'I want to take my fiddle and play a tune for the little Holy Child and his Mother,' he said to himself. 'The little Jesus doesn't look very happy. I'll play Him a tune - a real Christmassy tune all for Himself.'

95

So there stood Simon, his fiddle under his chin in the half darkness, playing away to the little Christ-Child on Mary's knee. A dim light nearby lit up the Nativity scene and made it seem very real. Simon played merrily away, and his music echoed round the quiet church.

And then something happened. Simon looked up – and the roof of the church was no longer there. Big stars shone above his head, hanging in the velvety sky. Simon stopped playing, feeling startled.

He looked round him. Where was he? He wasn't in the church any more. He was on an open hillside, and not far off were the dim shapes of huddled sheep. A little fire burned nearby, and men were clustered round it, their cloaks pulled close, for the night was chilly.

'Shepherds?' said Simon, under his breath. 'Shepherds and their dogs! Glory be to God, what's happened to me this Christmas night?'

And then suddenly the sky was filled

with a bright light, so that Simon was almost blinded. He gazed up, blinking, to see what it was. In the middle of the light were dazzling beings – hosts and hosts of angels! They were singing beautifully, singing a song that the world was to hear for centuries afterwards.

'Glory to God in the highest! Peace on earth, goodwill towards men!'

The shepherds fell down on their knees. They were afraid. Simon knelt too, but he put his fiddle under his chin, and, quite softly, he played the music to the glorious song the angels sang over and over again. 'Glory to God in the highest, peace on earth...'

Nobody heard him, not even the shepherds. Simon listened and played, happier than he had ever been in his life. He was playing for the angels' song, but they didn't know. What wonderful music!

Then the brilliant light faded, and the hillside became dark. Simon could see nothing at all after the dazzling light. Then gradually a little light came back - but it wasn't the light of the stars - it was the light from the little lantern hung in the church near the Nativity scene. Simon was there again, and on Mary's knee the tiny Christ-Child smiled and looked happy.

Simon went on playing the music of the song he had just heard. He played it softly, over and over again. He wasn't clever enough to write it down - but he knew it and he could play it!

Nobody believes the old man, of course, except the children. He tells the tale to them over and over again, and then he plays the angels' song. If only I could hear it too!

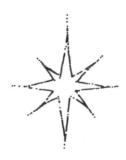

9

*A Shock
for Mister Meanie*

It was cold weather, and Mister Meanie's old dog didn't like it. Mister Meanie wouldn't let him sleep in the house, so he had to sleep outside. He wouldn't have minded that at all if his kennel had been warm. But it wasn't.

There wasn't enough straw in it for one thing. And it faced the cold north wind for another. Old dog Trotter shivered and shook each night, but he couldn't go and curl up in a warm hedge because he was on a chain.

'Couldn't I have some more straw, Mister!' he would whine, when Mister Meanie went out in the morning. But Mister Meanie had never been good at understanding dog-language as some people are. So he didn't bring any more straw to old dog Trotter.

When the frost grew harder, Trotter's water froze. Trotter couldn't understand it. What had happened to his nice wet water? It wasn't wet any longer, it was dry and hard and cold. Trotter felt very thirsty indeed.

'Couldn't I have some water?' he whined to Mister Meanie next day. But his master didn't understand a word, and never even noticed the frozen bowl.

One day he forgot to give Trotter his dinner. Trotter usually had a warm dinner, and how he looked forward to it. It warmed up his old bones and made him feel quite happy for a little while.

But that day Mister Meanie forgot all about his hot dinner, though old dog Trotter reminded him three times. He whined piteously, but Mister Meanie

didn't understand. The old lady next door threw him a bone, and that was all Trotter got for two days.

That night the frost was harder than ever and the north wind blew hard into Trotter's kennel. He had a round barrel for a kennel, so the wind got in easily. Trotter curled himself up at the very back, trying to pull a few wisps of old straw round him. But he couldn't possibly go to sleep because he was so cold, thirsty and hungry.

He shivered so much that his kennel shook and creaked. A small pixie, on her way to a meeting, heard the noise and came to see what it was.

'Trotter! Why are you shaking your kennel like that?' she asked. 'You are making such a noise.'

'I don't mean to,' said Trotter, glad to see someone who understood his language. 'I can't help it. I'm so cold that I shiver and my shivering shakes the kennel. Ooooh! I'm freezing!'

The pixie went inside. 'It's as cold in here as outside!' she said. She touched

Trotter's body. 'Oh, you poor thing, you feel as cold as ice!'

'I'm so hungry, too,' said poor Trotter. 'I keep thinking of hot gravy, and warm stew, and biscuits and bones, and things like that. And I'm thirsty. Something has happened to my water. It's gone hard and dry.'

'Why, it's frozen!' said the pixie. 'Oh, Trotter, I can't bear you to be so cold and hungry and thirsty. I really can't. Where's your master?'

'In bed, I expect,' said Trotter, shivering again. 'He doesn't understand my dog-talk, Pixie. I keep telling him how cold and hungry I am. It wouldn't be so bad if he would turn my kennel away from this cold wind.'

'I'm going to help you,' said the pixie. 'I am on my way to a meeting, and I'm going to go there and tell everyone about you. And I'm going to bring them back here, and we'll soon shift your kennel round! I shan't be long!'

She ran off in the frosty moonlight. She found all her friends waiting for her at the meeting-place, and she quickly told them about Trotter. They were sorry, and came back eagerly with her.

It was hard for such small folk to move the big, heavy barrel, even though Trotter got up and stood outside whilst they did it. But at last it was done. With scrapings and creakings it was swung to one side, so that the cold north wind no longer swept into it. Trotter crept in. It felt warmer already!

'Now we'll get you some straw, and some water and some food!' cried the pixie. Off she went with her friends, but there was no straw to be found anywhere. Nor was there any water, for every puddle was frozen hard. They could not find any food for Trotter and they came back, sad.

'Never mind,' said Trotter. 'I do really feel a bit warmer now I'm out of the wind.'

'Let's get into Mister Meanie's house,' said the pixie, to the others. 'There's sure to be warm bedding there and we can ask him for food and drink for Trotter.'

So they crept into the house. Mister Meanie was in bed, snoring so loudly that even the pixie's shouts did not waken him. She pulled and pinched him with her tiny hands, but he did not move.

She stood looking up at him. 'What a mean, unkind face he has!' she said to the others. 'I don't like him. I wish Trotter didn't belong to him. Look at all the lovely, warm blankets he has – and his poor dog didn't even have a handful of straw to keep him warm!'

'Well, let's take his blankets for Trotter!' cried one of her friends. 'We can tug and pull till we get them off!'

This seemed rather a joke to the pixies. So they began to tug and pull, and the blankets slid off Mister Meanie to the floor. The pixie opened the front door, and the little folk dragged the warm blankets out to Trotter's cold kennel.

'Here you are, here you are!' they

106

cried, and piled them all round the shivering dog. How delighted he was!

'I've never been so cosy in my life!' he said, burrowing into them. 'Now I shall be warm!'

The pixie ran back into the house to look for water. But they could not turn the taps because they were too stiff for them. So they went to the larder and found a big jug of creamy milk.

'This will do!' said the pixie, and between them they managed to carry the heavy jug out into the yard. They emptied the milk into the bowl and called Trotter to come and drink.

He got out of the warm blankets and padded eagerly to the bowl. He lapped thirstily, and did not stop until he had finished every drop of milk.

'I never enjoyed a drink so much before!' he said. 'Never! Milk, too – what a treat!'

The pixies forgot to take the empty jug back with them to the larder. They left it in the yard. They went back to the larder and looked for something for Trotter to eat.

'Here's a big meat-pie,' said the pixie. 'And look, a joint of beef, already cooked! Let's take those to Trotter. He'll be pleased.'

Was Trotter pleased? He was much more than pleased. He just simply couldn't believe his eyes and nose! He gobbled up the meat-pie in a trice. Then he took the big joint of meat in his mouth and began to chew it.

'Oh, it's good, it's good!' he cried. 'Excuse my talking with my mouth full, but I can't help it. It's so good!'

A cock crowed in a nearby yard. 'We must go,' said the little folk. 'Good-bye, Trotter. We'll come and see if you are warm, and have something to eat and drink, to-morrow night. We won't forget you.'

109

They went off, leaving Trotter to finish the joint. Then the happy dog crept back into his warm blankets, and snuggled down in them, sleeping warm and cosy for the first night for weeks.

Now, the pixies had left the front door of Mister Meanie's cottage wide open. The wind swept in. His bedroom door was open too, and as he had no blankets over him he soon began to feel cold.

He was so cold that he stopped snoring and woke up. He reached out for his blankets, which he thought must have slipped down. He couldn't feel them anywhere. He sat up and put on the light.

'I suppose my blankets are on the floor,' he said to himself. But they weren't. Mister Meanie looked everywhere, feeling most astonished. 'Where have they gone?' he kept saying. 'Brrrr! How cold it is! Where can that freezing wind be coming from?'

He thought he would get up and go downstairs to heat himself some milk. Then perhaps he would feel warm again. And maybe a slice of meat-pie would make him feel better too.

He was astonished to find the front door wide open. 'Can thieves have been in and taken my blankets?' he wondered. 'My, how cold I am! Where's that jug of milk? I'll heat it up.'

But the big jug of milk wasn't there. Nor was the meat-pie! And the big joint was gone too. Mister Meanie stared round the larder in great dismay.

'Thieves and robbers! Blankets gone
– jug of milk gone – and meat-pie and
joint gone! What am I to do? I shall
freeze in bed, and to-morrow I shall
have no food but a loaf of bread!'

There was nothing to be done but to
go back to bed hungry, thirsty and
cold. He wrapped his old coat round
him, but that didn't warm him very
much. And then the thought of old dog
Trotter slid into Mister Meanie's mind.

Trotter hadn't even an old coat to
keep him warm. Nor a handful of
straw. And how cold that wind must be
to-night, outside in the yard!

Mister Meanie half thought of going
out into the yard and calling Trotter
into the house. But he didn't.

The next morning he went out to see
Trotter. Imagine his surprise when he
found the old dog curled up in blankets
– the blankets from his bed!

And there, beside the kennel, was the
empty milk-jug – and not far off was
the empty meat-pie dish – and dear me,

was that the bone from the joint of meat? Yes, it was!

Mister Meanie stared and stared. He thought hard. It wasn't burglars that had come in last night. It couldn't have been Trotter himself, for he was on a chain. It couldn't possibly have been the policeman because he would have wakened up Mister Meanie, and told him to look after his dog himself.

And somebody had shifted the kennel round so that it was now out of the wind. Mister Meanie began to feel very uncomfortable.

Who was it, that came into his house at night, and took his blankets, his milk and his food, and gave them to his dog? He felt ashamed, too when he remembered that Trotter had no warm straw, and that he had forgotten to give him water and food.

'I must have my blankets back,' he said to Trotter. 'They're my only ones.' He took them away - but he slipped Trotter off his chain, so the dog was able to run about and keep himself nice and warm.

When he came back from his run he found that there was fresh water in his bowl, and biscuits mixed with hot gravy in his dish. Oh, good, good, good! Trotter wagged his tail, and gave Mister Meanie's hand a lick. Like all dogs, he was very forgiving indeed.

Another surprise awaited Trotter when he got into his kennel. It was filled with good, fresh straw, warm and cosy. 'Ha! This is even better than blankets!' said Trotter to himself, and began to make himself a kind of den in the middle of the straw.

'Trotter,' said Mister Meanie to his old dog, 'Trotter, listen to me. I don't know who it was that fed you last night, or gave you my blankets. But you might ask them not to do it again, because I'm ashamed of forgetting you, and I never will again. Do you understand, old dog?'

Of course Trotter understood. He wagged his tail hard, licked his master's hand, and gave a few joyful barks. And dear me, for once Mister Meanie understood dog-talk, and smiled. I don't think he will forget old dog Trotter again, do you? And I shan't forget *my* dog either, on a cold and frosty night!

10

The New
Little Milkman

There was once a little boy whose father had six cows. He sold the milk that the cows gave him, and made quite a lot of money. He had a small black pony and a neat little milk-cart that took the milk round to all his customers.

Now Freddy, the little boy, often used to go round with his father and the pony. It was fun to give out the milk to old Mrs. Lacy, and young Mrs. Thomas, and Mr. Timms, and all the rest.

Freddy knew all the customers, and said 'Good morning' to them in just the same cheerful voice as his father's.

Somebody else often used to go in the little milk-cart too – and that somebody was Tinker, the big puppy dog. He belonged to Freddy, and he was such a big clumsy thing, so loving and gay. Freddy loved him very much indeed.

Freddy made himself a little milk-cart from a big wooden box. His father put some wheels on it and a shelf all the way round for milk-bottles. The bottles were only toy bricks, of course, because his father wouldn't give him real bottles.

Freddy had to be the horse and the milkman too.

'I'm the galloping horse!' he told Tinker, and he stamped his foot on the ground. 'I'm taking the milk round. Hear me go clip-clop, clip-clop. Now here I am at old Mrs. Lacy's. Now I'm the milkman. Good morning, Mrs. Lacy. A pint of milk to-day? Here it is. Thank you. What a fine morning it is!'

Then he took hold of the handles of his wooden cart and was the pony again. Tinker watched him and thought that Freddy was wonderful.

Then one morning a great idea came into Tinker's head. Why shouldn't *he* be the horse? Couldn't he pull the cart for Freddy? Of course! And then Freddy could be the milkman, and stay at the back of the cart, instead of sometimes being the horse and sometimes the milkman.

So the next time that Freddy played at being the milkman, Tinker ran to the cart and put himself between the two long handles. Freddy gave a shout when he saw him.

'Tinker! You're the cleverest dog in the world! You really are. I can see you want to be the horse. All right, you shall be! I'll get a rope for reins, and tie you in properly.'

So before long Tinker was harnessed to the wooden milk-cart, and the two of them went round the garden together, stopping whenever Freddy said he had

come to somebody who wanted milk.

'Mr. Timms! How much milk to-day? Good morning to you! Mrs. Jenks? I'm sorry, I've no cream at all. I'll have some eggs to-morrow.'

120

It was a good game to play. Tinker and Freddy never got tired of it. Sometimes they both went in the real milk-cart, and then the two of them watched and remembered every single customer, so that they might play the game properly.

One day something horrid happened. Freddy's father went out with his pony and milk-cart on a very frosty day. The roads were slippery, and as thcy went up High Hill, the little black pony slipped and fell. The milkman ran to help her up, and she kicked out as she tried to rise.

Quite by accident she kicked Freddy's father on the leg. Poor man! *He* fell down then, and the passers-by had to come and pick him up. His leg was badly hurt – and the poor little pony had a hurt leg too.

'Well, this *is* an upset!' said Freddy's mother, when the milkman was carried home, and the little black pony was shut up in her shed, having limped all the way home with the milk-cart.

121

'What a good thing you had delivered all your milk!'

'Maybe we shall both be better to-morrow,' said the milkman, lying back in bed. 'You can milk the cows, can't you, my dear? Freddy can help. He's a good little lad. See to the pony for me, and get the doctor to him too, if he needs it.'

Well, the animal doctor said that the pony was not to walk for a week, or he would be lame for the rest of his life. And the milkman's doctor said that he too must lie in bed for a week or more, or *his* leg would not get better either.

'And *now* what are we to do?' said Freddy's mother to Freddy. 'I could take the milk round myself in the cart if only the pony was all right. But I can't possibly carry all that milk myself. Besides, I don't know the customers.'

Freddy stared at his mother and his heart began to beat fast. He had thought of a perfectly wonderful idea.

'Mother! You and I will milk the cows

and bottle the milk,' said the little boy. 'And then *I* will take the milk round in my little wooden milk-cart.'

'Oh, Freddy dear, don't be silly!' said his mother. 'You can't drag all that milk round by yourself.'

'I'm not going to,' said Freddy. 'Tinker can do that. You've seen him playing at being my pony, haven't you, Mother?'

'Well, I never! What ideas you do get!' said his mother, laughing. 'And do you really suppose you could get all the milk-bottles into that little cart of yours, Freddy?'

'No, I couldn't,' said Freddy. 'But I could keep coming back for more.'

'But you don't know all the houses where Daddy takes his milk!' said his mother.

'Yes, I do,' said Freddy. 'I've often been with Daddy and I know everybody. Really I do, Mother. Do let me try.'

'Well, I really don't see how we are going to get the milk round,' said his mother. 'I'll let you try. Freddy – just take a few of the most important people their milk. There's Mrs. Thomas, with her five children – she really *must* have her milk. And there's old Mr. Harris. He's ill and has to have lots of milk too. You must take his as well.'

Well, you can't imagine how excited Freddy felt! He ran to tell Tinker.

'Tinker! Just fancy! Our game of pretend is going to be REAL!' cried Freddy. 'What do you think of that?'

Tinker wagged his big tail and jumped around in glee. He was always pleased when Freddy was happy.

The cows were milked next morning. The milk was put into clean bottles – big bottles and little bottles. Then Freddy ran to get his cart. He carefully put the bottles into it. He could only get fifteen in, but that didn't matter. He could easily come back for more!

Then he harnessed Tinker to the wooden milk-cart. Tinker was pleased to be a real pony this time, with real, heavy milk-bottles to pull along instead of wooden bricks.

'Good-bye, Mother, we're going!' shouted Freddy. And off they went. Tinker clattered out of the farmyard with the wooden cart behind him, and Freddy ran behind the cart, clicking to Tinker as if he were a real horse.

They stopped at Mrs. Lacy's. She opened the door, surprised. 'Why, I thought there would be no milk this morning!' she said. 'I heard about the accident. Dear me – what a marvellous boy you are, to be sure! You've got a milk-cart and dog-pony of your own! I'll have a pint of milk, please. Here's the money. And tell your mother from me that she's got a fine, helpful little boy!'

Freddy grinned happily. He put the money into a bag. Then he set off for the next customer, Mrs. Thomas. She was waiting for him anxiously.

'Oh, Freddy! I was so afraid I would get no milk for all my children this morning!' she said. 'What a good boy you are! And I do like your horse and

cart. I must find a biscuit for the horse.'

She gave Tinker a biscuit and he munched it up at once, wagging his tail so hard that he almost knocked a bottle over in the cart. Freddy was given a chocolate and the money for the milk.

He went on to the other customers. He knew them all, and didn't miss a single one out. He had to go back home three times to fill up his cart again with bottles of milk. He sold it all, and took his mother the money. She counted it out.

'Exactly right!' she said. 'Well, I never knew before what a sensible, clever little boy you are, Freddy! And as for Tinker, he's a treasure! I'll give him a bone at once!'

So Tinker had an extra large bone, and Freddy had a large piece of ginger cake and two peppermints. He went to see his father and told him all about the morning.

'Thank you, Freddy. You *are* a help!' said his father. 'I was afraid I should lose all my customers this week, but I see I shan't. You and Tinker are fine.'

Well, Freddy and Tinker worked very hard all that week until the milkman and the little black pony were both better. Then, the next Tuesday, the pony was put into the real milk-cart again, and the milkman himself drove off with all his bottles of creamy milk.

'I'm quite sad that we're not the milkman and his horse any more,' Freddy told his mother. She smiled at him.

'Well, you can be my errand-boy, now,' she said. 'I want to buy a few presents for a kind little boy I know. Will you go and choose them? Take your cart with you, and ask Tinker to pull them all home for you. I want you to buy a packet of chocolate, a bottle of sweets, a new kite, and a story-book. Here's the money.'

'Who are the presents for?' asked Freddy, astonished. 'Is somebody having a birthday?'

'No,' said his mother. 'The presents are for *you,* of course! Daddy and I are very grateful to you for your help, you see, and we want to give you a reward. Oh, I've forgotten something. Buy a new ball for Tinker, too. Now, off you go!'

So off went the two of them, as happy as could be. And what a time Freddy had choosing all the things and bringing them home in his cart. But he did deserve them, didn't he?

11

Because My Mother Does

The children were all working hard one afternoon at school, when a big black cloud came over the sky. The rain fell in enormous drops.

Then there came a crash of thunder, and a flash of lightning. Some of the children screamed.

John crawled under his desk at once. Annie fled to the darkest corner of the room. Jill tried to get into the handwork cupboard.

'A storm! thunder! lightning!' yelled Peter, looking pale.

Miss Brown rapped on her desk. 'Children! A storm is nothing to be afraid of. It's a grand sight, a wonderful happening. John! Whatever are you trying to crawl about on the floor for?'

'Because my mother does!' said John, in a small voice. 'She gets under the table or under the bed.'

'Annie! Why are you hiding away there in a dark corner?' called Miss Brown.

'Be-be-cause my m-m-mother does!' said Annie, in fright.

Then Miss Brown looked at two children who had gone to the window to watch the magnificent storm sweeping over the country.

'Kenneth! Hilda! Why have you gone to the window to watch?'

'Because our mother does!' said Hilda. 'She loves the brilliant lightning and the way it lights up everything for a second and then is gone. She loves the massed-up purple clouds. She makes us laugh about the thunder-crashes. She says somebody must be spring-cleaning

133

up in the sky, and rolling heavy furniture about. There goes a wardrobe tumbling down the stairs!'

The crash of thunder at that moment really did sound like wardrobes falling down a flight of stairs. It made the children laugh, and even Jill came out of the cupboard.

'You have a sensible mother, Hilda and Kenneth,' said Miss Brown. 'Now – all those who want to be sensible, too, and see the grandeur and magnificence of a storm, come to the window with me! There's nothing to be afraid of except your own foolish fears!'

Every child but Annie and Jill came to the window with Miss Brown. John stopped crawling about the floor and came, too. After all, if nearly everybody went to watch the storm, it must be all right! Soon he was marvelling at the flashes of lightning, the rolling clouds and the rumbling thunder. It was grand and exciting.

When the storm was over, Miss Brown made the children sit at their desks again. 'Before we start work again I want to talk to you,' she said. 'First of all, Annie, Jill and John, what did you say when I asked you why you fled away in fright at the beginning of the storm?'

'Because our mother does,' said the three.

'And why do you suppose your nice, kind mothers are afraid of storms?' asked Miss Brown. 'They are not cowardly, are they?'

'Oh, *no,*' said John. 'Mine once jumped into a river to rescue somebody who was drowning. I know why she is afraid of storms.'

'Why?' asked Miss Brown.

'Because *her* mother was,' said John.

'And I've *seen* granny in a storm. She's really terrified.'

'Why?' asked Miss Brown again. 'Why should your granny be so afraid of storms?'

'I know why, because she told me,' said John. 'It's because *her* mother was afraid of them and used to rush

135

screaming into the darkest cupboard when the thunder began. And when granny was a child and saw her mother doing that, she really thought the thunder would eat her or something, and she rushed to hide too. And she does still. And so does my mother.'

'And so do you!' said Miss Brown. 'John, isn't it queer? You rush to hide in a storm because your mother does. She does it because her own mother did. And her own mother did it because *her* mother did. And so there is a long chain of fear, just made out of copying somebody else!'

The children laughed. 'I'm afraid of beetles – but only because my mother is!' called Lucy.

'And I'm terrified of cows – but only because my mother runs away when she sees one!' called out Katie.

'And I scream when I see a bat – not because a bat has ever hurt me, but because my mother always screams when she sees one!' said Rita.

'Well,' said Miss Brown. 'I had a

mother who loved thunder-storms, and kept mice for pets, and milked cows every morning, and thought beetles were comical little things – so, luckily for me, I too like storms and cows and bats and beetles and mice and all the rest. I suppose there isn't a chain of fear in my family. Now, children – put up your hands all those who are afraid of something, and whose mothers are afraid too – all those who have a chain of fear in their family.'

Nearly all the children put up their hands.

'Look at that!' said Miss Brown. 'Now boys and girls, what about breaking these chains? What about passing on to our children a love for storms and cows and tiny mice, instead of a fear? Can you do it, do you think?'

'*Yes!*' shouted all the children, even Jill and Annie. Now that they all saw that their fears just came from copying somebody else's fright, it seemed easy to break the 'chain of fear,' as Miss Brown called it.

137

'Good,' said Miss Brown. 'I'll ask Farmer Straw if he'll let us watch the milking each Saturday and each take a turn at it with the cows. That will break any *cow*-fear we've got.'

'And I'll bring my pet mice to school and we can all take turns at looking after them,' said Harry. 'They are so tame. They will even sit in my hand.'

'And we'll study beetles and earwigs and bats in nature study,' said Miss Brown. 'We'll have a lovely time. And if we haven't broken those silly chains by the end of the year, I shall be surprised!'

Well, will you believe it, long before the end of the year not one of Miss Brown's children were afraid of anything. Instead, they loved the magnificence of a great storm, they enjoyed milking the cows, they all had pet mice, and they got so interested in the beetles and earwigs they kept to study at school that a good many of them kept them at home, too.

'We've all helped one another,' said Miss Brown, 'and your children will be glad, and will say, 'I've got a sensible mother – she isn't afraid of anything, so *I'm* not, either.'

Are you afraid of anything, just because some grown-up is? Well, you break that chain. You can, you know!

12

Jack Gets a Chance

'Mummy, I don't like the boy next door to us,' said Janet.

'Nor do I,' said Paul. 'I saw him throwing a stone at our robin this morning. Fancy throwing stones at a *robin*!'

'He's always throwing stones at birds,' said Janet.

'Well, why don't you tell him what you think about it?' said their mother.

'Well, you see – he's not the kind of boy you can tell things to,' said Janet.

'I mean – he'd just go and throw *twice* as many stones if I or Paul told him not to.'

'Oh, I know the kind of boy,' said her mother. 'He will only do things if he himself wants to, and not if anyone else tells him. Very difficult. Usually those children are rather stupid and just won't learn.'

'But, Mummy – we simply must stop him throwing stones at our robin,' said Paul. 'Suppose its leg or wing was broken!'

Their mother thought for a few minutes. Then she spoke to the two waiting children. 'Now listen,' she said, 'the only way to teach boys like that is to let them teach themselves. So I've thought of a plan.'

'What, Mummy?' asked Janet. 'You're always so good at plans!'

'The birds in our garden are tame,' said Mummy, 'because in the summer we give them water to bathe in, and in the winter we feed them. I am sure that sooner or later Jack will notice how tame the birds are here, and ask you why. Then you must offer to tame his for him, too, on condition that he doesn't frighten them away at all, by throwing stones or anything, till they really *are* tame!'

'But, Mummy – how dreadful to tame his birds and then have him being unkind to them!' cried Paul.

'I see what Mummy means,' said Janet, slowly. 'Mummy – you mean that once you get Jack to look out for the birds to come to a bird-table, he'll not want to throw stones at them and frighten them away.'

'Yes,' said Mummy. 'There's a chance that Jack is more silly than cruel, more thoughtless than unkind. We'll give him a chance, shall we?'

The children weren't at all sure about it, but as they felt certain that Jack would never stop throwing stones just because they ordered him to, they thought they had certainly better try Mummy's way.

Two days later, when Janet was

Jack Gets a Chance

digging in her garden, with their robin close by, watching for worms, Jack's head popped up over the wall.

'I say!' he said. 'Look at that robin. It's almost on your foot. My, if I could get them as close as that to me I could hit them every time with my stones.'

Janet wanted to say something angry but she didn't. 'It's easy to tame birds,' she said. 'Paul and I can always tame as many as we want to.'

'However can you do that?' asked Jack, astonished. 'Could *I* tame them? Could I get them to come near? I'd have some good shots at them then.'

Again Janet had to stop before she spoke because she felt so angry. She dug hard for a moment or two and then spoke.

'Paul and I can show you how to tame the birds,' she said. 'We can show you how to bring them close to your window.'

'I say! I wish you would!' said Jack. 'That's the bother about birds – they will never come close enough for me to get a good aim at them.'

'Paul and I are going to put up our bird table to-morrow,' said Janet. 'If you like, we'll come in and put one up for you, too. That will bring the birds close to you. But it's no good us doing that if you start to throw stones at them as soon as they come. They'll just fly away and *never* get tame.'

'Oh, I'll wait till they're properly tame before I throw at them,' said Jack. 'Why, I might get them so tame I could catch them!'

'Last year we had a robin that took biscuit crumbs from our fingers,' said Janet. 'Now, Jack – is that a promise? Do you really and truly and honestly promise that you won't scare the birds away at all till they are quite, quite tame?'

'Oh, yes, I promise that all right,' said Jack. 'I can be very patient when I like.'

Janet went in to tell Paul and Mummy what she had said to Jack. 'But, oh, oh, Oh, how I hate him!' she cried, stamping her foot. 'Horrid, un-kind boy! Oh, Mummy, do you really think he won't want to throw stones at them and hurt them if he gets to know the birds? Are you sure? He seems so very stupid and unkind.'

'We'll give him a chance,' said Mummy. 'It is good to give people chances. But if they don't take the chances we give them, then they must be given punishments instead. We'll see if Jack will take his chance.'

Next day Paul and Janet went into Jack's garden. They carried a pole, to make a leg for the bird-table, and a flat piece of wood for the table itself.

'It's quite easy to make,' said Paul: and he drove the end of the pole into the ground, hammering it in with a mallet. Then he nailed the flat piece on top. It was very near to Jack's window. Jack could almost touch the table by putting his hand out of the window.

At the back of the table Janet nailed some branching twigs. 'The birds like to perch on those sometimes before they land on the table,' she explained. 'Now have you got a little dish for water, Jack? The birds like a drink, and often they come for a bathe, too.'

'I've got an enamel dish that our dog had once,' said Jack, and he filled it with water and put it on the table. 'Now, is there anything else to put on?'

'Well, food, of course!' said Janet. 'You'll have to put some on each day, Jack. Can you do that?'

'Oh yes,' said Jack, who was getting quite interested in his bird-table. 'I can put some bread on – and anything else you say.'

'Can you hang a bone from one end of the table?' asked Paul. 'The tits will come for that. And if you could shell some nuts and hang those from the table on a thread they will like them, too. And I can give you some seeds from the store I have for my pigeons. Some of the birds prefer those – the chaffinches, for instance.'

'What a lot you know,' said Jack. 'Well, thanks very much. I'll do all you say. And I'll keep my promise to you, and won't scare the birds away at all till they're so tame I can hit any one of them I want to!'

Janet went red with trying not to lose her temper. Paul said nothing. They soon went back to their own garden and put up a fine table for themselves.

They saw that Jack was putting out food each day. They saw that he had hung up a bone and some nuts. He kept the dish of water filled, too. But at first no birds came. What! Go to a table in the garden of a horrid boy like Jack. No, they didn't trust him at all.

Then a sparrow or two flew down and pecked up some crumbs. The robin flashed down and back again. A tit had a look at the bone.

'They're beginning to come,' Jack shouted over the fence. 'I say, what's the bird with a pretty, rosy chest?'

'Chaffinch,' said Paul. 'Fancy you noticing that.'

'Oh, I notice things all right,' said Jack, looking pleased with himself.

148

'Well, see if you notice a bird, quite a big one with freckles down his front,' said Janet. 'That's one of our thrushes. And you'll be sure to know the black-bird.'

Next day Jack appeared over the fence again. 'I saw your old Freckles. And do you know, *two* blackbirds came. And, I say, the robin bathed in the bowl. He sent drops of water all over the table.'

'You *are* lucky to see that,' said Paul. 'No bird has bathed in our bowl yet. Have you seen any of your birds sip the water yet, Jack? They're so funny to watch.'

'No, I haven't. I'll watch and see,' said Jack. And the next time he called out in glee. 'Well, I've seen my birds drink. The thrush took a big drink. He put his head in, took some water in his beak, then held his head back and let the water trickle down his throat. I never knew birds drank like that before.'

Then the tits came in crowds to

Jack's table, and he sat at the window watching them. He was amazed at their ways. 'They're acrobats!' he said to Paul and Janet. 'Real acrobats. They stand upside down on my bone, and they swing like anything on the nuts. Honestly, I could watch them for hours.'

'If you want to see something *really* funny put a bone *on* your table,' said Paul. So Jack did this, and to his great amazement six or seven starlings flew down, and began to squabble and squawk, and push each other about like a lot of naughty children. How he laughed at them.

'The bird I like best is the little robin,' he told Paul and Janet. 'Hasn't he got fine, big, black eyes? You know, my robin's so tame now I believe he'd take a biscuit from my fingers. I'll try him.'

After about three weeks Paul spoke to Jack about his birds. 'They're as tame as ours,' he said. 'All except the little robin. I must say you're a great success with the birds, Jack. They come to you as much as they come to us.'

'Yes. I've noticed that,' said Jack. 'I bet they'll sing loudly for me in the springtime.'

That afternoon one of Jack's friends went to tea with him. Jack asked Paul and Janet, too. After tea they sat at the

window and looked at Jack's bird-
table. It was full of birds.

'I say!' said George, Jack's friend.
'Where's that little toy gun of yours,
Jack? We could shoot all those birds as
easily as anything. Or what about
going into the garden and finding
some stones? I'd like to throw one at
that fat thrush.'

Jack stared at George in surprise.
'What! Hurt my birds! Shoot my gun at
them! You must be mad, George! You

don't suppose I've tamed them all these weeks just for you to shoot at, do you? Don't be so beastly.'

Now it was George's turn to stare at Jack in surprise. 'But, Jack, what's happened to you? Have you forgotten the times we went into the woods with your catapult? And how we threw stones at those woodpeckers, and the wild ducks on the stream? Come on, let's shoot your gun at those birds there. We'll never have them so close again.'

153

'You can go home,' said Jack, fiercely. 'If anyone hurt that robin out there I'd – I'd – bang his head as hard as I could. Go home, or else I'll fight you!'

George went at once, angry and puzzled. Jack turned to Paul and Janet, who had been sitting quite quiet, listening. 'Isn't he hateful?' said Jack. 'You don't blame me for losing my temper, do you? I felt like slapping him.'

'Yes. We know how you felt,' said Janet, 'because, Jack, we felt exactly the same about *you* some weeks ago! We hated you, too! But Mummy said that if we gave you a chance to teach yourself about the birds, perhaps you would take your chance, and learn. And you have.'

Jack stared at her. He suddenly went red. 'Yes – I was awful, wasn't I?' he said. 'Worse than George, I suppose. I've forgotten how I felt about birds then – I just thought they were silly little things to throw stones at. Now I know them, and I love their funny little ways. I'm proud they are tame with me. I wouldn't scare them away for worlds!'

'Well, you make a bird-table for George, then!' said Paul, getting up. 'Make him change his mind, as you've changed yours. We played a kind of trick on you, Jack – and it's worked! We only pretended to be friends with you before, to see how our trick worked – but now we'd like to be *real* friends – wouldn't we, Janet?'

'Yes.' said Janet. 'We would. Let's go and tell Mummy about it all, Paul. She'll be so pleased!'

She was – and she told me to tell you that whether you love birds or not, it's great fun to make a bird-table. Do try it some day!

13

Five Times Five Are...

Little Hoppitty hadn't had at all a good morning at school. Mr. Rap was very cross with him because he couldn't say his five times table.

Hoppitty managed all right till he came to 'Five times five.' He *couldn't* seem to remember that they were twenty-five.

'Five times five are twenty-six,' he said.

Mr. Rap rapped on his desk with his cane. 'You said that yesterday, Hoppitty.

Now – tell me the right answer this time. What are five times five?'

'I *know* they are twenty-six,' said Hoppitty. 'It sounds right and it is right, Mr. Rap.'

'Now listen,' said Mr. Rap. 'Take twenty-six pencils out of my class pencil-box. That's right – twenty-six.

157

Have you got them and counted them? Now Hoppitty, if you are right, and five times five are twenty-six, you will be able to arrange five nice piles of five pencils, out of those twenty-six. But mind – you mustn't have any over'

'That's easy,' said Hoppitty.

'If you can do that I will put you at the top of the class,' said Mr. Rap. 'And that's a place you've never been in before. And if you're wrong – my word, I shall have quite a lot to say to you!'

Well, Hoppitty began to put the pencils into piles of five. He made five nice piles – and then he found he had one pencil left over. Bother! He began all over again – but, of course, no matter how he tried, he couldn't make five times five come to twenty-six – there was always one pencil left over.

'There you are!' said Mr. Rap. 'What did I tell you? Five times five are twenty-five, not twenty-six. Come up here and hold out your hand!'

Poor Hoppitty! It was a very painful way of learning what five times five were. He cried when he ran home from school. But on the way home he passed a curious little caravan standing by the roadside, and he stopped crying. Who lived there? He had never seen the caravan before. It just must have arrived!

Hoppitty tiptoed up to it. The door was wide open. Nobody was inside. On the shelves around the caravan were arranged little bottles of all colours.

'Bottled spells!' said Hoppitty to himself. 'Ooooh – I must just read the labels!'

He was reading the labels when suddenly someone came up the caravan steps – and the door banged loudly. Hoppitty turned round in alarm.

A little goblin woman stood there, with eyes as bright as green glass. 'Ho!' she said. 'What's your name? Is it Peep-and-Pry? Is it Snoop Around? Is it. . .?'

'No, no, no – I'm just little Hoppitty!' said Hoppitty in a fright. 'Let me go. My mother is a wise woman, and she

159

will blow a spell at you and make your caravan vanish like a puff of smoke if you keep me here!'

'She can't. I am much cleverer than she is,' said the goblin woman. 'Nobody is so clever as I am. There is nothing I can't do! You've seen my bottled spells – well, half the magic in the world is in those bottles!'

'My mother is cleverer than you,' said Hoppitty, beginning to tremble. 'She could ask you to do something you couldn't do. Let me fetch her.'

'Oh no! You wouldn't come back!' said the goblin woman. '*You* ask me something. Surely such a clever woman as your mother must have a clever son. Can't *you* ask me something I can't do?'

'Turn into a dog!' said Hoppitty. 'That's very difficult!'

It wasn't difficult for the goblin woman! In a trice she vanished, and in her place came a very fierce-looking dog that growled at Hoppitty.

'Now turn into a - a - cucumber!'

Five Times Five Are...

cried Hoppitty, trying to think of something that didn't growl or look fierce. At once a long green cucumber lay shining on the floor. Most peculiar!

The goblin woman appeared in her own shape again. 'I like you,' she said to Hoppitty. 'I shall take you along with me. You can pull the caravan when my horse is tired.'

'No, no!' cried Hoppitty. 'Give me one more chance. I know something you can't do, I do, I *do!*'

'Very well – one more chance,' said the goblin woman. 'Quick!'

'Well, have you got twenty-six pencils?' asked Hoppitty.

'Of course not,' said the goblin woman.

'Well – potatoes will do, I suppose,' said Hoppitty, seeing a basket of them nearby. He counted out twenty-six. 'Now see these potatoes?' he said to the goblin woman. 'Well, you're to put them into piles of five for me. You won't be able to do it.'

'A baby could do that,' said the goblin woman, and she quickly made

five piles of the potatoes, five in each pile ... but there was one over, of course.

'Oh, you mustn't have any over,' said Hoppitty. 'That's not allowed. You must just have piles of five with no potatoes over at all.'

Well, the goblin woman tried and tried, just as Hoppitty himself had tried at school that morning. In the end she cheated and put four piles of five and one of six. But Hoppitty saw what she had done.

'You're not only stupid, you're a cheat too!' said Hoppitty. 'Cleverest woman in the world indeed! What rubbish! Why, I expect all those bottle spells are just coloured water. I shall tell everyone you're not clever enough even to ...'

'Get out of my caravan!' said the goblin woman, fiercely. 'Go on, get out. I don't want you. You've played some kind of trick on me. You're too clever! Get out before I empty a bottled spell over your head!'

Hoppitty fled down the caravan steps and didn't stop once till he was safely at home. My goodness, what a good thing Mr. Rap had made him find out that five times five are twenty-five and never could be twenty-six! You just never know when a bit of knowledge will come in useful!

14

*The Boy
Who Borrowed*

Benny loved reading. He always had his nose in a book, and he never had enough to read.

'Really!' said his mother, 'you only take half a day to read a book, Benny! You need a book about as long as the dictionary!'

'I want a book that goes on for ever,' said Benny. 'That's the only book that will really give me enough reading!'

Benny hadn't enough money to buy a lot of books, and no one gave him any except at Christmas time. He had about eight of his own and that was all.

So Benny borrowed books from his

The Boy Who Borrowed

friends and from the library. 'Please will you lend me *The Island of Adventure*?' he asked Bill. 'I haven't read it.'

He asked Mary for *The Secret Seven* and she lent it to him. Then he borrowed *Five on a Treasure Island* from Henry and two nature books from John.

But – he always forgot to give them back! At least, he forgot at first – but when he saw his bookcase gradually filling up, he simply couldn't bear to give back any of the books. So he didn't. If the children asked him for them he pretended he hadn't got them. He was a most dishonest little boy!

He didn't only borrow books. He borrowed a ball from Eric, and a pen from Lucy. Kenneth lent him his jigsaw, and Eileen lent him her new rubber. He didn't give any of them back, and the children were very cross indeed.

And then one night something happened. It was something very pecu-

liar, and Benny quite thought it was a dream.

He sat up in bed because he thought he heard a noise. Surely there were voices in the other room, where he kept his books and toys?

Benny slipped out of bed. He listened outside the door of the room. Yes, there were voices!

'It's too bad!' said a voice. 'I don't belong to Benny. I belong to John. I've got his name inside me.'

'So have I,' said another voice.

169

'And I belong to Bill,' said a third voice. 'He loved me very much and read me six times. Now I'm stuck here in Benny's shelf, and I don't like him. He doesn't treat me properly either. He's turned some of my pages down to mark his place, and that's a horrid thing to do with books.'

'I belong to Mary,' said another voice. 'I was a birthday present from her mother and she liked me. Now I have to stay here, though I know Mary has an empty place in her bookcase, waiting for me.'

'Let's go!' said yet another voice. 'Why should we stay here? Let's run down the stairs and go to that little room where there's always a window left open for the cat. Come on! I won't stay here and be a borrowed book any longer!'

'Good gracious!' thought Benny, in alarm. 'Why, it's the *books* talking! Would you believe it!'

The door was pushed open. Books came out, pushing and jostling, eager

to get down the stairs. They walked over Benny's toes and didn't seem to notice him at all. He was too frightened to stop them or even to say a word. They tumbled helter-skelter down the stairs. They went into the little room off the hall and found the open window.

Then there was silence. Benny went back to bed, trembling. He didn't like it at all. He fell asleep - and when he awoke in the morning, he laughed.

'Oh, Mother!' he said at breakfast-time. 'I had such a funny dream last night. I dreamt that all my books went walking downstairs and ran away!'

'Well, well – what a queer dream to have!' said Mother.

But what do you think! When Benny went to get his school-books that morning, he found his bookshelves quite empty except for his own books! All the others had gone.

Benny sat down suddenly, because his legs felt queer. So it hadn't been a dream. It was real. It had happened. Those books he had borrowed had gone off in a temper, and left him. They would all be back with their right owners now.

Benny was so frightened that he didn't know what to do. Then he caught sight of Eric's ball and Lucy's pen. Suppose they did the same thing too! Why, they might even do it in broad daylight, and then how ashamed he would be!

Benny went very red. He collected

Eric's ball, Lucy's pen, Kenneth's jig-saw, and Eileen's rubber. He found some other things he had borrowed and put them all into his school-bag.

He handed them back to the other children. 'I'm sorry I kept these so long,' he said, in a small voice.

'Thank you,' said the children in surprise. 'We thought you meant to keep them!'

'That would have been stealing, really,' said Eric.

'Oh, Benny – thank you for sending back my book *The Boy Next Door*,' said Mary. 'I found it in my bookcase this morning.'

Benny stared at her. Good gracious! So her book had managed to find its way right to that empty place in Mary's bookshelf! The others told him that their books were back, too.

'I shan't borrow again unless I give back very quickly,' thought Benny. 'I wouldn't like this to happen to me again!'

I wouldn't like it either, if I borrowed

The Boy Who Borrowed

and didn't give back, would you?

15

The Wishing Feather

One day, when Snubby was walking along the road, he saw a pretty blue feather lying in the gutter. It had a red tip to it, and Snubby liked it.

'Just the thing to stick in my hat,' he said, and he picked up the feather and stuck it into his hat. He at once felt very grand indeed, and went whistling along the road. He didn't know that it was a wishing feather!

He passed by Dame Cooky's little shop. The plump old dame was just setting out some hot pasties in her little window. They did look nice.

'Look at those!' said Snubby, stopping. 'I do wish I had one to eat!'

Well, of course, as he had a wishing-feather in his hat, his wish came true. He suddenly felt something hot against his side, and he put his hand into his pocket in alarm to see what it was.

And in his pocket was a hot pasty! Well, well, of all the surprises! Snubby took it out and looked at it. 'I don't know where you came from, but I do know where you're going!' he said, and took an enormous bite out of the pasty.

But it was very hot and he burnt his tongue. He gave a howl that made Dame Cooky look up. She saw Snubby eating one of her pasties! Yes, there wasn't a doubt of it at all! She counted them quickly and there was one missing. Bad Snubby! Wicked Snubby!

She ran out of her little shop and snatched the pasty from Snubby's hand. He was most surprised, and very cross indeed to see his lovely pasty being thrown down into the gutter and stamped on by Dame Cooky's big feet.

'You bad little robber!' shouted Dame Cooky. 'Stealing one of my pasties and eating it under my very nose!'

'I didn't steal it! You nasty, horrid person!' cried Snubby. 'I wish you were in your oven, cooking with your pasties, so there!'

Well, of course, Snubby still had that wishing-feather in his cap, and in a trice Dame Cooky found herself back in her kitchen – and, oh my, she was being crammed into her hot oven with the next batch of her pasties.

How she yelled and screamed! Mr. Top-Hat, her next-door neighbour, ran to rescue her, and pulled her out of the oven at once.

'Do you want to cook yourself?' he said to her. 'Whatever are you trying to get into your oven for? Pooh, you smell scorched.'

'It's that wicked Snubby!' cried Dame Cooky, and she ran out into the road again. 'He wished me in my oven – and there I was! He's got hold of some magic somehow. We'd better catch him before he uses it on us all!'

Mr. Top-Hat and Dame Cooky pounced on Snubby, and shook him

hard. 'Where's the magic you are using?' they cried. 'Give it up at once!'

Shake, shake, shake! Snubby's teeth rattled in his head, and his eyes nearly fell out.

'I haven't any magic!' he gasped. 'I haven't, I haven't. Let me go! Take your hands off me! I wish you hadn't got any, you horrid things!'

Well, in a trice Mr. Top-Hat and Dame Cooky let go of Snubby – and, oh dear, they had paws instead of hands! Snubby's wish had come true. He stared at the paws, and so did they.

'My wishes are coming true,' said Snubby, in a loud voice. 'I don't know why. But they are. I'm powerful! I'm important! I'm grand!'

'Wish our hands back again!' wept poor Dame Cooky. 'How am I to make pasties with paws like these? Wish our hands back again.'

'Certainly not,' said Snubby. 'It serves you both right. My word, what a time I shall have, paying people back for horrid things they've done to me!'

'Wouldn't it be better to forget all that, and pay people back for the *good* turns they have done you?' said Mr. Top-Hat. 'When you have a bit of power, you want to do good, not bad, Snubby. Be careful, or you will be sorry.'

'Pooh!' said Snubby, 'you only say that because you want me to wish you back your hands. Well, I shan't. I'm going to enjoy myself now. Hallo, here comes Mr. Smack. Many a time he's spanked me. I'll wish him a few things to wake him up a bit!'

Mr. Smack came nearer. He was the village school-master, a learned and strict old fellow. Snubby let out a yell as he came up.

'Hallo, Smack! I wish you had a cane running behind you to make you hurry!'

In no time at all a long thin cane appeared behind poor Mr. Smack, and hit him very smartly indeed. Mr. Smack yelled and began to run. The cane hopped along, too, getting in a

The Wishing Feather

182

good old smack every now and again.

Snubby jumped about for joy. 'Now I wish a whip would come and crack round his ears!' he shouted. The whip appeared, and what with its loud cracking, and the whippy little cane, poor Mr. Smack had a very bad time indeed.

Then up came Dame Tick-Tock and Father Bent. Snubby greeted them with a loud shout.

'You scolded me the other day! Now I'll pay you back! You've got your best clothes on, and I wish you'd get wet through!'

Down came a shower of rain, just over poor surprised Dame Tick-Tock and Father Bent. How wet they were! It was a most surprising sight really, because no rain fell anywhere except just over the two astonished people.

Soon the word went round that Snubby had got hold of some wishing-magic, and was using it. Everyone came running to see what was happening. When they saw Dame Cooky and Mr. Top-Hat with paws instead of hands, and saw poor Mr. Smack trying to escape from the cane and the whip, and Dame Tick-Tock and Father Bent getting wetter and wetter, they were amazed.

'Now stop this, Snubby!' cried Mr. Plod the policeman. 'How dare you behave like this? I'll take you to the police-station and lock you up.'

Snubby roared with laughter. 'I wish a dozen policemen would run after you and try to catch you to take *you* to the police-station!' he said.

And then twelve big policemen suddenly appeared and went to put heavy hands on the astonished Mr. Plod. He began to struggle with them, and got away. They ran after him. Snubby laughed till the tears ran down his cheeks.

Then people began to feel afraid. Snubby certainly had got some kind of powerful wishing-magic, there was no doubt about it. And he was using it badly. There was no knowing what might happen if power was in the hands of a bad pixie who didn't know how to use it.

One by one the watching people crept away, afraid of Snubby, and scared of what he might do to them. Snubby saw them going, and he rejoiced to see how frightened everyone looked.

'Come back!' he shouted, and a great idea came into his head. 'Come back! I want to tell you something. I am very great and powerful now. I can wish for anything I want. I am the most important person in the whole of this town. I shall be your king.'

'You are not fit to be a king,' said Mr. Smack, dodging the whip that cracked around his ears. 'A king should know how to use power rightly and well. You don't. And you never will.'

'I wish for *six* canes behind you!' shouted Snubby in anger. 'Aha! They will make you jump. How dare you talk to me like that?'

Everyone was silent. Snubby threw out his chest and strutted up and down.

'I am your king. I shall have a grand, golden carriage. I wish for it now, drawn by twelve black horses!'

It came, of course. One minute it wasn't there and the next it was, a fine, gleaming carriage with twelve black horses that pawed the ground impatiently. Snubby climbed into it and sat himself down, folding his arms.

'I wish for a coachman and two footmen!' he said, and, hey presto! there they were.

'And now I wish for a golden palace with a thousand windows,' shouted Snubby, feeling tremendously excited. There was a loud gasp as the watching crowd saw a beautiful palace appear on the hill nearby. Its thousand windows glittered in the sun.

Snubby gave a shout of joy. 'See that?' he yelled. 'That's my home! And I'm your king! Bow down to me, all of you! Bow down or I'll turn you into black-beetles!'

Everyone except Mr. Smack at once bowed themselves low to the ground.

Only Mr. Smack stood upright, and the cane gave him a horrid little smack. Snubby pointed his finger at Mr. Smack, who had suddenly caught sight of the wishing-feather in the pixie's hat. 'Yes, there is no doubt about it,' thought the surprised Mr. Smack, 'that is a wishing-feather!' How had Snubby got hold of it? And did he know he had it? The cane gave him a swipe on the legs and made him jump.

'Hey, you!' roared Snubby, still pointing his finger at Mr. Smack. 'Bow down to me, do you hear? I'm your king.'

An idea flashed into Mr. Smack's quick mind. 'You are not a king till you wear a cloak and a crown,' he said. 'Where is your crown?'

'That's easy!' cried Snubby. 'I wish for a cloak and fine clothes, and I wish for a golden crown!'

Away flew his old clothes and in their stead came gleaming ones of red and silver. Away flew his hat and on his head came a glittering crown. '*Now*

I am your king!' cried Snubby to Mr. Smack. 'Bow down!'

Mr. Smack did not bow down. He watched the hat whisk away with the

wishing-feather in it. He knew what would happen when that was gone. All Snubby's magic would go. Ho, ho! What a shock for Snubby!

'If you don't bow down at once I'll wish you a pair of donkey's ears!' cried Snubby, in a rage, pointing his finger at Mr. Smack again. 'What, you won't bow? Then I wish you had donkey's ears on you!'

But no donkey's ears came. And suddenly everything began to change. The gleaming palace on the hill faded

into a mist, and all its thousand windows were gone. The lovely carriage faded, too, and Snubby found himself tumbling to the ground. The horses threw up their heads, neighed, and disappeared. The coachmen and the footmen vanished.

Dame Cooky's hands came back, and so did Mr. Top-Hat's. Dame Tick-Tock and Father Bent were no longer wet through. The twelve policemen who were after Mr. Plod faded away like shadows in the sun.

And all Snubby's fine clothes disappeared, and his crown as well. But his old clothes didn't come back, nor did his hat with the lovely wishing-feather. There stood poor Snubby in his holey vest and nothing else, shivering and scared. The wishing-feather was gone, and his wishes would no longer come true. He could do no more magic. He had used it so badly, and this was his punishment.

'All my magic is gone!' he wailed. 'There's nothing left.'

But there *was* something left – and that was the nasty little cane that had first come to annoy Mr. Smack. That hadn't gone – and now it left Mr. Smack and came hopping over to Snubby. Wheee! It gave him a fine blow and made him jump in the air! Wheee!

'Don't, don't!' cried Snubby, and fled away. But the little whippy cane followed him, and everyone laughed to see Snubby leap into the air every time he was hit.

'He could have wished a thousand good wishes,' said Mr. Smack. 'Now all that is left to him is one bad one. Ah, if only I had found that wishing-feather, what a wonderful lot of good I'd have done with it!'

I would, too. Wouldn't you?